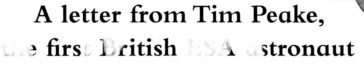

A letter from Tim Peake,
the first British ESA astronaut

(European Space Agency Principia mission
to the International Space Station, 2015-2016)

Dear Reader,

We are all astronauts, young and old, zooming around the
Solar System on our very own spaceship: planet Earth.

When I look up at the stars, I see the future – filled with
further space exploration and new scientific discoveries.
I see my two young sons looking up at those same stars,
and I remember experiencing the early feelings of wonder
and excitement that I now see on their faces.

Goodnight Spaceman is a delightful book that tells
the story of two children, just like my sons, who dream
of joining their dad on his adventures in space. I hope it
may inspire a new generation of boys and girls to look up
at the stars and not just ask questions but to go and seek
answers of their own.

Tim Peake

For Seth Lewis Waterfield - M.R.

For Finny J x – N. E.

PUFFIN BOOKS

UK | USA | Canada | Ireland | Australia | India | New Zealand | South Africa
Puffin Books is part of the Penguin Random House group of companies
whose addresses can be found at global.penguinrandomhouse.com.
www.penguin.co.uk   www. puffin.co.uk   www. ladybird.co.uk

Penguin
Random House
UK

First published 2016
This edition published 2016
001

Goodnight Spaceman

PUFFIN

Michelle Robinson

Illustrated by **Nick East**

It's time for bed, come on inside.
We'll keep the curtains opened wide
and watch the starlight sparkling bright.
Let's make a wish and say goodnight.

Goodnight shuttle.

Goodnight base.

Goodnight deepest, darkest space.

Zooming through the Milky Way . . .

Goodnight spaceman, far away.

Goodnight Daddy's rocket ship.
Time to go, enjoy your trip.
Five . . .
four . . .
three . . .
two . . .
one . . .

Astronauts:
please check your suits,

backpacks,

helmets,

gloves

and boots.

Just imagine what we'll find
when we leave our world behind.

Astronauts: prepare for docking.

Nearly there now,

doors unlocking . . .

"Come aboard and join the crew!

Pull the lever,
take it slow.

Goodnight light years in between us.

Rocket ships

and
shooting stars.

Goodnight

Mercury

and
Mars.

Final orbit past the moon ...

"Goodnight Earth, we'll be home soon."

One small step,

one giant leap.

Goodnight spacemen, time to sleep.